HEAR
MY
CRY

CALVIN OCKLETREE

OTHER BOOKS BY CALVIN

Thoughts of Suicide (COMING SOON)

MORE POETRY FROM LEXXIKHAN PRESENTS PUBLISHING

Somewhere Between Love & Misunderstanding

Not Just Another Angry Black Woman (COMING SOON)

DEDICATION

I want to dedicate this book to myself.

.

LexxiKhan Presents Publishing
www.LexxiKhanPresents.com

Ordering Information:
Quantity sales. Special discounts are available on quantity purchases by corporations, associations, and others. For details, contact the publisher at the web address above.

Calvin loves to keep in contact with his loyal supporters. Follow him online:

Instagram.com/trapofvibes

Or

TrapofVibes.com

ISBN-13: 978-0-9600635-7-4

CONTENTS

CONTENTS

CONTENTS

NOTE FROM THE AUTHOR

I don't know how vague or deep I want to be with my 'about me section' (in the back of the book). The reason being was because this collection of poems that you will soon devour, and at the leisure of your own personal perception, are more than enough to get to know me. So, I will leave you with some basics.

My name: Calvin J. Ockletree
Hometown: Indianapolis, IN
Favorite color: Red
Favorite Basketball team: Lakers
Favorite football team: Colts

Ok, I will stop being an asshole, but seriously, I do not want to ruin your journey on learning who I am through my collection of poems that address three focal points in my life that have shaped me into who I am today. I do want to lay a disclaimer out there for my female readers; I am stating here – now- that some of the poems that are listed under my chapter "My Cry to Her" are not recent feelings or thoughts that I practice or believe today. I found a multitude of poems that I have written over a course of twelve years and compiled them into a chapter by itself. Please, read with an open mind to what I am trying to capture within the work compiled here within, "Hear My Cry."

-CJO

PROLOGUE

HEAR MY CRY
This craft is not a joke to thee,
I live and breathe poetry.
When I lay my head down to sleep,
I dream of the lines that bleed from my aged pen.
I look around at the dilettantes that perform and imitate true souls that bear this burden.
They play with words and profess to have wisdom and falsely come to the aid of those who, in their weakest time, open their ears to be captivated by fallacies?
These Machiavellian Anti-Christs work hard to coincide in the kingdom of poets -
You act as a sycophant and believe that we do not notice your true character – a Svengali?
Manipulating the minds that your tongue loosely slips promises through their frontal lobes
Down the tubes that stream with their dopamine connecting to their adrenaline, pumping the blood to their hearts.
Do you recognize your damage?
Your manslaughter?
Your cruelty?

We true poets are looked at as the anomalies behind our own craft!
So, this is my Bravado.
I stand here letting you know that I am real; I stand weak in blunder, mentally strained
And cursed with this ability to surf my mental and put it down on paper,
I dream of thoughts and images that even my own conscious rejects from

memory.
Known for my imperfections and praised for my misery watched like a new specimen,
Peers waiting or the ticking to stop and for me to blow...
Standing in my own kingdom, nursing this burden that I bear
I look out to the masses, accepting the view... cut eyes that stare at me and judge
But in compliance I know I'm just misunderstood
So, this will be perceived as a stance of bravery or defiance?

You decide....

So, will this be perceived as a stance of bravery or defiance?

MY CRY TO SELF

This monster with lyrical steroids, deceptions with charismatic dressing… Lurking amongst crowds I realize this craft is not healthy; But I re-up on my own drug — infatuated with the temporary feelings. Such a repetitive act created an army of monsters just by bedding them, the craft, sent out to return the favor amongst my own kind. A legend in a sense… But not one that shall be remembered for his honorable acts. The Negro Hitler… spasms produced from the urge of destruction rerouted from its root function

HEAR MY CRY

MOTIONS

I cannot go back.
I cannot change my past.
Looking at the hourglass
Wondering how it still lasts.
Beaten and torn down by verbal destruction,
Still dealing with choices
I made from my original root function.
Bashed for rumors from the west but I cannot act as if I don't deserve this
Outcast on my chest.
I did not want this to come to fruition –
Be known as a savage bastard who salivates at tension,
Destroying dreams facilitated into situation-ships.
Hearts sold into slavery by my own mental instability
Being deemed crazy and wild by those near and far
No one has taken the time to understand that seriously something is wrong
with me.
I have allowed my inner turmoil to boil over and spill into my precious world
Curled and entangled into my own despair.
I stretch and reach for concealment and air.
Looking my heirs in the eyes
Asking why they have been placed into my generation of time
Only to recline
Reclaim the name
Of the picture-less frame
Tamed by the indigenous stain carved into my spinal chords
Downward lanes
Cranes built to suppress the pain
Bolted and looped around my muscles
Strained and unrested with no initial gain.

I still cannot go back and change my past.

Looking at the hourglass
Wondering how it still lasts
Beaten and torn down by verbal destruction
Still dealing with the choices I made from my original root function
Constantly on the run from my own emotions
Trying to omit the promotion of motions within my idealistic notion that my
life is not totally in commotion.

Looking at the hourglass
Wondering how it still lasts
Beaten and torn down by verbal destruction
Still dealing with the choices I made from my
original function
Constantly on the run from my own emotions
Trying to omit the promotion of motions within
my idealistic notion that my life is not
totally in commotion.

HEAR MY CRY

WHY THE CONSTANT DISAPPOINTMENT?

Lost on the road to my future feeling defeated, lack of motivation, stuck on my previous mistakes, baggage and heavy burdens molded into my mental wavelengths…

Why the constant disappointment?

Constant drama
Hearing so much negativity – I start to believe it is I.
This monster with lyrical steroids, deceptions with charismatic dressing…
Lurking amongst crowds I realize this craft is not healthy; But I re-up on my own drug – infatuated with the temporary feelings. Such a repetitive act created an army of monsters just by bedding them, the craft, sent out to return the favor amongst my own kind. A legend in a sense… But not one that shall be remembered for his honorable acts. The Negro Hitler… spasms produced from the urge of destruction rerouted from its root function.
In conjunction with spiritual warfare, casted by my own peers that lurk in the midst of my mental fog
As dogs return to their own vomit,
From the faithless hobbit,
Possessed.

Seasonal fellowship…I cry wolf… the bic strikes fire.
Inhale my African Ancestors
Exhale that diminished black culture that struggles to exist - terrorism at its best…
The devil is here to collect, the bureau of souls, proceed with the process of elimination, abominations born, nations scorned, mourning for the death count recorded in the mornings. Assassins basking in the blood of lost memories. But let's look at the hierarchical irony. I'm still lost on the road to my future feeling defeated, lack of motivation, stuck on previous mistakes, baggage heavy, burdens molded into my mental wavelengths.

Here I stand on a middle-class docket looking up climbing a ladder of despair.
Focusing on achieving what?
These false beneficiary accomplishments that are praised and accepted by society's standards?
Hell no.
I've dealt with that already on a minuscule level achieving in school, becoming a part of multiple upstanding organizations, joining a Noble Klan of Noble men. Being in the 'in crowd,' sitting at the high end with the most popular. Only to crash hard, Britney Spears, known as a legend, but judged

harshly.

Michael Jackson – criticized for his ways and beliefs.

Edgar Allan Poe – a genius with addictions.

Sigmund Freud – created an equation to life – Albert Einstein… But all of which great things were said regarding the negativity that haunted them, still they stood strong in the midst of adversaries… My hands will never be clean, all I can do is sacrifice myself. Modern day Constantine, hoping, feigning for that one true blessing. Throwing myself into known danger, the sweet line between accepting death and achieving salvation.

Lost on the road to my future feeling defeated, lack of motivation, stuck on my previous mistakes, baggage and heavy burdens molded into my mental wavelengths…

Why the constant disappointment?

BEFORE I LAY MY HEAD TO SLEEP

DEAR GOD,

It feels so right when I do wrong, and it feels so wrong when I do right.
Caught up in the worldly deceptions of happiness – bathing in my sinful ways,
Comfortable in my filth,
I am a totally different person.
Focused, but blinded by my own ambition.
I look at those around me.
I see mirrors reflecting the image of myself.
No one is perfect, but we judge those that are not our caliber of sinner.
You and I are NO DIFFERENT!

God,
I am not pleased with my actions.
I feel lost without you.
I need you in my life.
Every day I feel as if I am one step closer to hell.
My prayers don't even seem like they come to you,
Instead, they bounce right back down off the ceiling back to me.
My conscious is clouded.
My heart is cold, and my soul is diminished.
Is this how a child of God should feel?
I am so good at doing wrong and struggle doing right that I give up sometimes.

I hope that You have not given up on me.

We true poets are looked at as the anomalies
behind our own craft!
So, this is my Bravado.
I stand here letting you know that I am real;
I stand weak in blunder, mentally strained
And cursed with this ability to surf my mental
and put it down on paper,
I dream of thoughts and images that even my
own conscious rejects from memory.

HEAR MY CRY

<u>ALONE</u>

When I look around, it's on me not to feel alienated within my own community.

I think it's a fact to be stated that yes, I am well known amongst the masses.

But it's rare that you can find someone that truly understands me.

You want to make a move and stand to preach the complex identity that you possess,

But instead you think of the negative connotations that will be in response to your truthfulness.

A wise woman once told me that being able to stand alone and be yourself shows a sign of spiritual growth.

But being alone is not that easy.

Walking around behind my veil, stuck in my mind, asking questions of approval.

How am I perceived?

Why would you want to be me?

Where are those that get me?

How much longer do I have to deal with this feeling?

Annexed from Central Society but a common factor that is involved with our everyday task.

I came into this world alone and will leave this world alone.

But honestly,

Who wants to do that?

Locked in my own mind I'm masterminding and building nerves of steel, it's about the only place that I can save from being invaded.

It would be apparent that the fault shall fall upon myself if I allow something to invade my thoughts.

But I cannot help but think of those around me who send words of interest to my frontal lobe

Making it seem so accepting, but it's neglecting my well-being

Instead it is their personal gain of information that might satisfy

Critical response with a twisted denouement

Yearning blistering tenuous strains from bloopers signaling to the community fallacies from the government of corrupted collegiate critics.

Gimmicks centralizing their position to fuel the fist of imposters that hide subliminally

Reconstructed through the mouth of takers-simple reporters that release null hypothesis based on their conjunction of beliefs.

I'm wishing the others would digest instead of regurgitating acts of chivalry

For the simple fact of a fair war between two ponds

I did not want this to come to fruition –
Be known as a savage bastard who salivates at
tension,
Destroying dreams facilitated into situation-
ships.
Hearts sold into slavery by my own mental
instability
Being deemed crazy and wild by those near and
far
No one has taken the time to understand that
seriously something is wrong with me.

HEAR MY CRY

Collection plate of glass, nails, needles; still sleeves rolled, I am the master of my fate.
Our hands briskly thrown in a 90° angle and forcefully dipped into a plate of pain
Withdrawal leaves us with a bloody aftermath
Collaboration in moderation
Ships taking sail without relation
Basing communication off of association
Clinging to friends that are enemies
I would rather die misunderstood
So, bless me Lord.
You knew my purpose from the separation of the umbilical cord.
Came in by myself, so I'll take my last breath by myself.

Here I stand on a middle-class docket looking up climbing a ladder of despair. Focusing on achieving what?
These false beneficiary accomplishments that are praised and accepted by society's standards?
Hell no.
I've dealt with that already on a minuscule level achieving in school, becoming a part of multiple upstanding organizations, joining a Noble Klan of Noble men. Being in the 'in crowd,' sitting at the high end with the most popular. Only to crash hard, Britney Spears, known as a legend, but judged harshly.

HEAR MY CRY

BREAD THAT HAS YET TO RISE

Trying to adapt to this new feeling
Wondering what actually has changed.
Have I grown at all?
Is it only in physical traits?
Mental strength is always on my to do list.
Tsk Tsk
Waiting for God to make the ultimate alterations
My life is strictly in the forward lunge
Reaching by day and night for the holy spirit.
It sucks living in this lukewarm environment.
This visual effect on the temptations that know you so well,
But the homestretch to recover seems so far away.

Is this how a child of God should feel?
I am so good at doing wrong and struggle doing
right that I give up sometimes.

I hope that You have not given up on me.

HEAR MY CRY

<u>COLD TURKEY</u>

Have you ever gone cold turkey?
Detached yourself from something
When the withdrawals start you close your eyes tight and try to forget
Instead waves of emotion burst into life, running circles around your mind
You can taste it.
Smell it.
Feel it.
A freak of nature, how much lack of control we have over our conscience.
So, what do you do?
Return to the effects that affected the cause for you to take action?
Drowning in mental pain – so hard to focus – no gain – lost in a maze of
frequent impulses that attack your heart and soul.
This addiction was no ordinary addiction – stronger than any drug.
Going cold turkey was not the plan, but the abrupt decision that rose to the
occasion.
That blue haze, that blinded feeling walking into the sun, that constant itch
behind your ear, shoulder and neck. Hoping for relief, but the only thing that
can help is time.
And at this moment, TIME is not on your side.

THE DARKEST HOUR

When you are down and out with no means of escape, what will you do?
Will you push through any hardships without expectations?
Blood, sweat, and tears fill the gravel around you on the journey as you progress
Dripping slowly causing dry spots to form where it used to leak continuously.
What will you do when you are cornered with no friends, no money, and exhausted from spiritual battle?

Watching the war still unfolding around you, you think to move, but the earth below is bound to worldly deceptions.
You wear a mask of bodily fluids, tasting the dehydration in the salt like form that pours down your face; Push forward.
Don't feel the restraint from the forces that work against you.
Mind over matter.
Mind over matter.
Mind over matter.
Mind over matter…

Do not give in to the pain, which is only weakness leaving the body.
Even when you feel that you have completely broken, push yourself further.
Prioritizing in prevention for the control of your freedom with great effort to succeed in conquering this task; so, serve this time that has you in bondage, but don't quit.
Don't quit.
Don't quit…

<u>VANTAGE POINT</u>

Anger pumping through my veins frontal lobe is discombobulated, trying to release prayers, straining to surpass my questioning conscience.
Mental hazing inflicted upon myself.
So caught up in my sinful ways, I do not notice the light surrounding my soul is fading.
Volcanic soot, a dark and deep shadow begins to form around me.
Fallen deep within the grasp of Hell's Kitchen, no longer do blessings pour upon me, but those burdens weigh down on my body EXHAUSTED!
Not from the everyday stressors of life but exhausted from the spiritual defeat.
Internal turmoil, transforming into the unthinkable.
I have become one with my demon struggling to regain control.
I need help.
I want help.
I want to ask, but instead I'm worried about how you judge me already.
Walking bomb exploding.
I fight this battle within.
Still, I receive hateful looks with whispers behind my back, and rumors that spread faster than a virus.
I fall back into my shadow where my soul has made itself comfortable.

Do not give in to the pain, which is only
weakness leaving the body.
Even when you feel that you have completely
broken, push yourself further.
Prioritizing in prevention for the control of
your freedom with great effort to succeed in
conquering this task; so, serve this time that
has you in bondage, but don't quit.
Don't quit.
Don't quit...

HEAR MY CRY

PERSONAL THOUGHTS

Staring into the wild
All things crossed my mind.
The smells of nostalgic settings
Zoned out in a trance
Standing still a loft of emotions
Lost on a journey of thoughts
Memories relived for the moment
Tragic, humorous, painful experiences
Spring into my cerebellum only to fall desperately in the pit of my soul
Out of control – I begin to sculpt my spirits
In its mold are the trials and tribulations from years old
Tapping into my conscious, tapping into that Winter cold
Bold and strong, cautious and accepting
Traveling amongst the waves in my mind
No gravity – surfing in the abyss
Everything fades away
Time zone unknown
Wishing the best for the future
Wonders of tomorrow
Where will I be led on the road to success?
Life moves like a game of chess
Mentally speaking
I'm moving on the coast
Never settling for inside the box
I draw lines through the equal sign
Poking holes in minds
Stretching the rules of matter of fact.

I have become one with my demon struggling to regain control.
I need help.
I want help.
I want to ask, but instead I'm worried about how you judge me already.

HEAR MY CRY

PATIENTLY WAITING

Does my work ethic go unnoticed?
The hours and time dedicated to the cause
For years I have watched others receive blessings
That they did not deserve
I started to question the purpose of doing right.
Right by people, right by the law, right by myself
Judging the behavior of others, whether right or wrong,
I saw no difference.
So long I had tried my best to be the good Samaritan
That upstanding citizen, a son to be proud of, a father to honor,
But even they have been shot down.
Those I hold close have mocked the attempts
Family and friends along with associates and enemies did their share of
torture and disconnect with my true self

Have I been fooled?

When I have gone wrong, I still struggle, going back-and-forth about what
to do
Tired of not knowing
My mind works against itself.
I dream of solutions but produce destruction.
I plan for success and disregard it in seconds.
Exert energy into quick satisfaction
But grow lazy when the true work is to be done.
Maybe I've become my worst enemy.
I fight myself daily.
I used to be easy to anger.
Now, I watch my anger linger in the shadows in the marsh
Eyes floating like a halo on top of the grassy fields
Waiting for me to signal to self-destruct.
I spend time on myself
Only to be broken back down
To see how much I have truly learned and adapted
Perfection stressed to the max
I can only hope that the Almighty has a purpose for this soul within me
I lay to sleep – watching yet another day pass by the same as before.
Patiently awaiting that call from above
Strung out on orders
Falling victim to repetitive actions.

<u>FEARS</u>

My deepest fear is becoming a failure, but I am seeing now that it attaches itself to another.

I am afraid of my own success.

I am afraid to use my talents and branch off into a world of endless opportunities.

I write night and day about anything and everything, but my purest and most rare form reveals itself when I'm with spirits simply tapped into a place no other could possibly understand.

Locked in position, pen bleeding onto blood drenched notebook paper. I sit outside myself and instruct my mind to unleash the restraints I have on my soul.

And afterwards, I awake with a blank mind and a piece of poetry to which I know not how it came to exist.

I remember beginning to write but the words of my conscious tell a story that I myself would not tell.

So, I try to forget these particular pieces, but they draw me nearer and nearer building the curiosity to dig deeper with the craft. Only to become obsessed with the unknown, holding all this in - I still have chosen to take it on as a burden. But I'm afraid of its true power.

I'm afraid of what it will make me become.

The control of oneself becomes lost in the craft I have yet to master, but it grows stronger within me.

It beats my heart drum like a tribal celebration you can hear miles away. I awake in the middle of the night in puddles of sweat and pray that my dreams were that of my imagination, but I open my palms with the urge to write what felt so real...

Living in fear is what keeps you living your true destiny within your dreams and they will haunt you until you release them.

<u>LOST</u>

He is lost in this pit of death.
The curse of a pathological liar dwells on his breath
With his silver tongue dreams are shattered.
With those shriveled lips self-esteem's, egos are battered.
O' those staggering burdens that live within his chest.
His pride stands tall with a sinful shadow,
Lukewarm trials leave him no means of winning this battle.
Accepting the infectious demons to influence God's cattle
For he wrestles with flesh and blood
Accepts the influence of principalities, deceptive powers, rulers of his dark pit
Spiritual wickedness in high places!
His body is a vessel of filth, broken bones, diseased skin,
But to the naked eye he is white as snow.
Born a sinner, raised a sinner, in the deepest corner of his heart is where sin continues to grow.
He tries to live a spiritual life, but in reality, he is living a lie.
But without God's gratefulness,
His new beginning, he cannot start.

I dream of solutions but produce destruction.
I plan for success and disregard it in seconds.
Exert energy into quick satisfaction
But grow lazy when the true work is to be done.
Maybe I've become my worst enemy.

Hear My Cry

MOSHI TIME

There is a force stronger than nature.

Twenty three years young I feel as if there's something that weighs down on my soul, initially yielding at defeat being decomposed by the lack of faith and preserved by consistent larvae that gave birth to rotted roots, which produce vines that lurk amongst the structure of my very own existence.

At the point of no return- simply wanting life to cease – never knew I would go this far

Potential not only a blessing but a burden that cripples me to believing that it will come without hard work and dedication

GINA & ALICIA EFFECT

I sacrifice my soul to this Holy Trinity. I constantly baptize myself into being reborn and I revert back to Gina and my horns grow.

She is everywhere I go…Everything that I crave.

Sometimes I dream that Gina is what's going to put me in a grave.

Begging for grace

Only to turn around and feign for the next taste.

Gina comes over constantly and randomly through the day or night and it's only seconds before I indulge in her flavorful strike.

Was introduced to her in an unruly manner only to become an animal seeking the same salvation of damnation.

When I slide into Gina, I transform into another life form – unlike anything seen before…

The good Lord looks down upon me while I'm in darkness feasting upon Gina.

Oxymorons upon blasphemies being uplifted in rebellious harmonic sounds from her host's vocal cords.

Even when bored, quick reliefs of stress bound by acidic and liquid outburst keep me occupied during all the drama and hardships that follow my soul into the snake pits of Gina's jaws.

Clenched tight with the venomous sedition of heavenly ecstasy molded around the shaft.

All mental awareness is routed on the physical embrace of the two entities.

Not knowing how Gina arrived to take this effect on my being, I try to recall the beginning of the evening when Alicia arrived with the rest of my friends.

Shots in honor of their arrival and Alicia goes around and touches the spirits of all those in the room.

Arising the different emotions of lust and meaningless affections, Alicia and I are a dangerous combination and I started hanging around her during family events at a young age.

We kept in contact from time to time connected at a few kickbacks here and there.

Freshman year of college we met again in Alabama and boy did it get toxic.

Limits never set – drowned in ignorance with sloppy decisions, which led to embarrassing memories. All chalked up as freshman year shenanigans.

No one judged nor worried – nothing to set off an alarm.

Alicia and I were in love and the thing that really shocked most: Alicia never tried to come between the relationship I had with Gina (the perfect situation)!

Alicia never tripped about being my side bitch and often I would try to get rid of her, but she still kept a heavy hold on me.

As the years went on, Gina and Alicia had a strong influence on my life.

Whenever I tried to branch out and settle with just one woman – the ladies would always tell me, "I have too many hoes."

Caught a couple that understood the situation-ships I had with them; but Gina, being as jealous as she was, would always find a way to interfere and run the good ones away.

When this happened, I would fall back on Alicia, and she would leave me on a late afternoon or evening of emotional rollercoasters.

So, I would call up Gina and tell her to come take the edge off.

The cycle was the new 'Calvin Cycle.'

Hell, plenty of folks could relate to me and if not, had their own version of Alicia and Gina.

He is lost in this pit of death.
The curse of a pathological liar dwells on his
breath
With his silver Tongue dreams are shattered.
With those shriveled lips self-esteem's, egos
are battered.
O' those staggering burdens that live within
his chest.
His pride stands tall with a sinful shadow,
Lukewarm trials leave him no means of winning
this battle.
Accepting the infectious demons to influence
God cattle
For he wrestles with flesh and blood

HEAR MY CRY

<u>PROCRASTINATION</u>

We only can see as far as the retina allows us to.
Worrying about tomorrow, procrastinating during the present, and then regretting the past
Utilizing current events as excuses of why we don't proceed with dreams.
Living in a constant quicksand of thoughts
Declining the advancement of growth
Outgrowing oneself – experiencing the same pivotal climax
Lost on a road of comfortable circumstances.

SPIRITUAL PAIN

Nothing gained from the environmental mainframe
Broken and restricted from salvation's release
Left to fend amongst the unknown
The uncertainty of tomorrow
The dangerous lapse of viewing other success
Drenched in sitcom reflections of your own life
The slightest pinch of hope seeps into the corridor
Only to be robbed of that temporary relief
With news that strangles your dreams by the neck
Lost on the green pasture with thoughts of what's next
Quick surge of painful energy interrupts the darkest day

I AM MY WORST ENEMY

I am my worst enemy.
Subduing myself with my personal pleasures
Digging the hole deeper and deeper
Creating reminders that stick
Playing devil's advocate with my greatest potentials
Questioning my ability to succeed
I am my worst enemy.

Living behind a veil of secrecy
Too many lies to cover my true identity
Afraid of being oneself for the good standing here at this university
Only to realize that truly is not me,
I am my worst enemy.

Friends that claim to be loyal to me
Associates that thrive off of my sorrows
A sea of people that may not be there tomorrow
How hollow does the bullet need to be?
So, my heart can break its ice and beat for me -
I am my worst enemy.

Lost on a road of darkness where I keep pissing on the candles that those
who truly care for me try to keep lit
Pushing and shuffling through my wildest dreams
I'm looking in the mirror and not recognizing who stands in my own skin
But I am me and no one can steal that from me
But what does that mean if I am my worst enemy
And I cannot commit to myself to make change?
Motivate myself to do better?
Where is the true confidence that dwells in my soul?
What does it mean when you're disgusted with your own self?

I am my worst enemy.

So much anger and pain
Within this child of the world
As silence fills the room
I awaken from my dream
And decide to choose
Not to no longer be my worst enemy

Friends that claim to be loyal to me
Associates that thrive off of my sorrows
A sea of people that may not be there tomorrow
How hollow does the bullet need to be?
So, my heart can break its ice and beat for me
-
I am my worst enemy.

HEAR MY CRY

MY CRY TO HER

THE ENCOUNTER

Looked into the eyes of the previous ended case
The beauty was stunning
But the exact lock of eye contact between us opened the dark holes that were
really there
Was it hatred, pain, sorrow, anger?
I will never know
For the two entities have moved on with their present focus.

HER NAME IS JOURNEY

On this road
I walk aimlessly in the mist of my future
The imagery of my past
Unnaturally presents itself as memory
An index
Scrolling through the dates
Aloft in time, picture snapshots vividly appearing as polaroid
Now traveling light, everything can fit in one basket
Shoulders feel lighter and my breathing is leveled
Trying to pace myself from the normality
Which now the abnormal expectations of this trip is expected of me
Fighting for direction on this path which is less traveled
Physically stuck in traffic, mentally locked in place, but spiritually the
destination has already presented itself.

Patience is a virtue.

But the flesh is weak, vessel in park, debating on clicking the hazard lights,
To decide whether to turn around or keep pushing forward.
Then, that destination looks me in the eyes, and it refocuses on my souls'
secrets and deepest desires.
The positive that exists within that puzzled vessel on this road of abnormality
Is possessed by purity… she exists…

Confused at the task ahead of me, I cannot decode this journey before me.
Lost amongst a road that is truly dependent on trust and intuition,
Locked and ready still willing to fully submerge my spirit within the shadow
of her voice
Guided by mere attraction
Blind from direction but acceptance of expectations I still accept this journey
Yes, indeed, I have come to realize the duties of me…
I want to follow through.
I will follow through.
I have to follow through…
I need this…
I want this…
I'm tired of driving a planned course of action…
What risk have been taken for that success?
I want more, and I need more.
I have traveled to the cities of understanding and lived amongst the norm,
But I have yet experienced the journey that has been presented to me.

Now is my time to take advantage of the right vantage point…
The one that I do not fully comprehend, the destination that does not speak my language
The area of purity that recognizes my kind from afar and up close can smell the stench from whence I came.

What an honor to be accepted on this journey…

My mind is blocked from the easy route to this destination, but still I persist in a manner of desperate need…
I am locked in…

TRUST ISSUES

Emotions thrown into a frenzy of dictating chaos
Control freak demanding access to my heart's deepest secrets
Knowing I have bottomless trust issues
Steadily keeping the velocity leveled between you and I
Still I press constantly against your love's current
In need of stationary grounds – but bound to loops of rollercoaster rounds
Bearing a crown – Lord of Flies- Throne of Trojans from past mistresses
Approached by true love – neglecting the perfect view.
What is it one may see that is so captivating to thee?

Multiple tries – golden coins inserted into my hearts arcade
The Game Era – mimicking the repetitive acts of charades
There is nothing to describe this feeling that I am feeling.

I trust no woman due to the plotted tragedies carried out by the black widows
from before.

I'm all day with this attitude – all night surfing amongst different altitudes
Afraid to put the time into a heart that accepts me but rather put the time
into the pussy that engulfs me.
I dwell in the nocturnal dimensions of insanity
Branded into this dark fraternity of not trusting these bitches
Tattooed on my flesh it's written as a statement to those who think of
attempting to know me
Running on this highway of déjà vu
Catch 22's of locking eyes with previous ended cases
Dirty remarks, snarling looks
That used to be hooked on my façade of gentleman characteristics,
But let's look at the forensics.
Deep into the scientific mental equilibrium of our souls Pandora
Flipping – back tracking – reminiscing – nostalgic from the victim's aurora
I'm blamed for being a K-9.
Operating my control center, selfishly reclined with just my feelings on my
mind.
Why be long-suffering with one who can destroy my nervous system and
govern over my soul's mentions?
Out of body experience trampling over letters of purity expecting me to be
serious
Clearly devoted to my personal great expectations
Resenting those who collide with my match button.
Clocking in and out with bitches that want to fuck,

But it is just my luck that every blue moon I run into a worthy candidate.
But my blind ambition leaves the decision unmade for me,
I stand alone subletting my emotions into the wild.
Living lavishly with my trust issues and Valet Park the pure one that leaves context clues
Back and Forth with the identity of who I am, bits and pieces of me spread across the universe.
I see myself in you, her, and them.
To many physical connections with bondless combinations
Relentless confusing relations
Rising complications with the external whispers ready to brew
Master mind behind the introduction phase
Louisville slugger when it comes to achieving second base
It's too late by the time she figures out it was staged.
All this to say....

I think we should just be friends and pretend that this is going to be a mutual understanding
Hoping that it does not backfire on me.

Am I harsh or am I smart?
To each their own opinion,
But if trust is what you want from me, your request is pending.

DEATH TO LOVE

The discoloration is painful
Black and white rusts into a dull grey
Anatomical position
The body is weak and breathless
In need of a seeker
Sought out by vultures
Inclined with hope
Pressure on the lungs
A gasp for air is released
In a motion of matrix
Eyes close with one last flutter
Downward spiral
Sending vibrations of potential energy
Cupid's bow of love was plucked
In return a life has been deemed less.

Master mind behind the introduction phase
Louisville slugger when it comes to achieving
second base
It's too late by the time she figures out it
was staged.
All this to say….

I think we should just be friends and pretend
that this is going to be a mutual
understanding
Hoping that it does not backfire on me.

Am I harsh or am I smart?
To each their own opinion,
But if trust is what you want from me, your
request is pending.

HEAR MY CRY

5 SENSES

The smell of sweet tea crawling up the cavities of my nose
The beauty that fills my pupils of the goddess before me
The taste of her works of agriculture that engulf the space of my stomach
Listening to her story that is condensed into a portfolio of chapters
When we touch its magic, no other feeling other than that nostalgic scene of
when our bodies intertwined

These are the 5 senses that she powers just with her spirit.

SIGNIFICANT PROTOTYPE

So as one of my idols would say, I have met yet another prototype,
But there is something different about this one.
Can it be that I see so much of myself in her?
Can it be that I feel her inner spirit?
Can it be that I simply want to mend a heart that is broken?
Strong willed, opinionated, head strong, sophisticated petite bundle of pure raw personality
One can only hide so much before it pours out through their aurora.
I sense that she is tired and through the mature species that she is, she is looking for something that is in our day and age nonexistent.
Time after time we as people make mistakes no matter what we may already know.
This only discourages us and creates insecurities that may affect us from moving forward in life, which leaves us stuck in neutral.
She focuses on observing others, while she neglects the recognition that she leaves her own personal door unlocked for someone to look deep into what truly lies within that thick membrane she calls, "Tough Skin."
So, what may be my purpose in her life — all I know is that I am going to teach her something new, introduce her into a culture that she has only dreamed of but that will take her breath away.
Oh, I see the full, complete potential that someone else might not, as the old saying goes, "someone else's trash is someone else's treasure."
It seems as if she has been treated to past relationships that were 80/20 and she got the piss poor performance, but I simply offer her a better fraction of 50/50 to only give her my best in hope that she gives the same in return.
The angelic presence of her around me lifts me in a positive manner, but I see deep within her and see that she is the one that needs to be lifted. She once called me a King, but I only hope that she knows that a Queen she shall be treated as under every circumstance.

She deserves the best…

So, baby I now speak directly to you…
You don't have to be afraid; I understand and see your pain.
I see your worries and doubts. I can promise to keep it 100 with you no matter what.
Your search is over. I promise…something just for you on the spot…

<u>MY OWN</u>

I needed something different.
We live in a world without love and not loving each other
A past failure of my heart once told me that it would take a special species of
a woman to love and aid my heart.
The key would be delicately made. Lined with her deepest desire to please
my every need. The handle would be coated with the loyalty of her soul to
me,
And as she begins to enter the key into the frozen lock and turns the key,
She would bring life back to a hollow object – out of commission for ages.
Now, revived by this new breed.
What is to come – neither knows. Neither looks back. Never to think of the
past. Everybody has an addiction,
Mine just might start to be you.
Everyone has an opinion, but there's only one that matters and that's entitled
to you and me.
Separated by miles connected by technological wavelengths.
Times that I catch glimpses of your face
Favoring any moment of time well spent
Future never seemed so bright.
In due time, I will rename this new breed of woman, and it shall be "My
Own."

I needed something different.
We live in a world without love and not loving
each other
A past failure of my heart once told me that
it would take a special species of a woman to
love and aid my heart.

HEAR MY CRY

<u>IS THIS DÉJÀ VU?</u>

This must be déjà vu between you and me.

Traveling in different dimensions – conducting frolic behavior within different dominions – crossing paths through different portals

Living out lifetimes with each other through the blessings of reincarnation.

Time capsules injected into our blood stream

Buckets of dreams achieved together.

We sold our souls to be and exist forever.

Bringing me near the brink of a new invention

The tension of our lips touching – the sweetest kiss.

Multiples of 9 by the representation of a divine intervention.

Luxury amplified by 10

Due to the consistency of our love.

Polished crystals reflecting the scenes of our history and the glare blinding the outside entries plotting their coin inserts.

Deferred obstacles opposing our final goal to become whole

Initial plans of dying by your side – Romeo and Juliet flow.

Promised to never let go- my memory will go with you being the last sight of my spirits addiction

Tempting the power of the universe – uncovering the truth of existence within the bind of becoming one with you.

This must be déjà vu between you and me.
Traveling in different dimensions – conducting
frolic behavior within different dominions –
crossing paths through different portals
Living out lifetimes with each other through
the blessings of reincarnation.
Time capsules injected into our blood stream
Buckets of dreams achieved together.
We sold our souls to be and exist forever.

HEAR MY CRY

THE SEASON OF THE MORTAL AND GODDESS

That fulfillment of adrenaline that rushes through our veins,
It's that hunger of sex that drips into our bottomless souls.
Oh, I wish you could connect with me now
Only so I can write my poetry
On the skin of your body with my tongue, so that you can feel my deepest thoughts.
Is it possible for a man to touch a Goddess, the mere mortal touch that I can offer, hopefully it shall suffice?
I only long to please you my highness.
Lift my sexual spirits high in the air
Let our deepest lustful thoughts burst into flames
Let me lick you in such a way that the winter raises the hair on your neck.
Let me lick you where only the sun shines between your thighs as if springtime has touched fresh daises.
Let the heat rise between our bodies – mimic the graze of summer loving…
As the leaves drown in the gravity of Fall, let the lukewarm feeling of my shaft burry itself deep into your four walls.
Oh, is it possible for a mortal to touch a Goddess?
If so, grant me all the power of MAN to please you…

Oh, is it possible for a mortal to touch a
Goddess?
If so, grant me all the power of MAN to please
you...

HEAR MY CRY

FORBIDDEN LUST

Have you ever had a great distance from someone that you felt so close too?
Forbidden from communication.
Forbidden from their touch.
Forbidden from their soul.
The forbidden fruits that laid in front of us.

Naked bodies standing across from each other – our eyes gaze with lust upon one another.
The heat rises and the sweat begins to drip down the crease between her breasts.
Her eyes glisten in the light that beams on her thick figure.
We anticipate each other's move – driving our minds crazy.
Wanting to grab the most exotic fruit.
Hoping that it will signal a sign for one or another to make a move.
Instead, the chains around our wrist and ankles remind us that we are forbidden from this lustful love.
Our sex drive has been abused and left unpleased for a time too long.
We are fuel to our own fire – flames bursting with sex positions – hot flashes of me having my way with her in any way.
Addicts of our own produce, producing fumes that could catch any one's animalistic nature and turn it wild.
No longer tamed, the sex driven couple pulls at their restraints.
Adrenaline pumping into the veins connecting to the dopamine in our brains–
Driving our nervous system into a power surge, the potential energy quickly turns into kinetic energy and the centripetal force oozes out of our pores.
Understanding that there is only one cure to our disease and that is to satisfy our desires with uniform action.

Spreading our arms abroad, we reach for each other's fingertips, interlocking them reaching deep within our lungs for one last breath.
Inhaling deeply – we lock eyes and simultaneously we pull with all our strength.
As our bodies fall upon the table in front of us,
The instant excitement rushes through our spines and raises the hairs on our necks…
Temporarily shocked, we look at the chains that use to hinder us from this forbidden love.

As we come to the realization of our freedoms,
Nothing but lustful cravings come to mind.

We strike each other with force and sincerity
Scratching, biting, pulling, slamming, choking, wrestling, slapping, caressing
each other with no intention on ceasing.

Feeding each other fruits of our labor,
We have both eaten from our forbidden fruits.
Juices run all over our bodies, the smell of wine and yeast cover us in full.
No room for excuses
Understanding that we shall be judged
Criticized by the masses we shall be
After indulging in each other's spirts.
We lay entangled – 69 fumbles into play
Tickling each other with our tongues in the most sensitive places.
Praising her body, running my tongue in circular motions around her holy
grail, whispers of untold legends couldn't be more prominent at this moment
in time.
As her body arches in a 45-degree angle, and the sound of a discrete yelp
attacks the silence of moans…

She crowns me king with her pussy upon my face as I bless her with a queen's
gift of head.
Spreading her thighs amongst my shoulders and resting her utter wettest walls
upon my cheeks
She falls weak to my tongue's touch yet again.
As her body shakes, and slowly comes to a halt, as her nails draw blood from
my back, she lets me know I win…
She lays across my chest and notices my smile and we burst into laughter.
Not worried about the critical votes from our outcast,
We enjoy each other sexually and there's nothing in this universe that can
defuse our lustful energy.

FIRST ENCOUNTERS

Spirits crossing the platonic membrane of new beginnings
Jolts of energy on the up rise
Colors spring from the musical vibrations conducted from the vocal cords
Blessing the frontal lobes of each other
Nevertheless, as random as it may be
Everything is harmless.
No stress.
Relief to exhale nothing heavy on the chest
Hopes of no games

All are too well infused with the mental spirals of chess
Exchanging views on life, relationships, two critics at their best
Often reflecting on personal and previous trials and tribulations
Combining thoughts joint at the hip in hopes of a relation
A rare bond being formed between two strangers
Crossing several medians
Transferring the means
Allotting the codes switching to the best modes
Sometimes these strangers lift the biggest buried burdens
Simply someone needs to listen and judge not.
Casting of No Rocks
The blind leap of trust
Softening the crust as the conversations stretches deep into the night
The moonshines dull on the light mist
Circling the two organisms
Sharing time in minimal afflictions
Of what's to come of this unique connection.

What motive drives the curiosity between the two?
Notary stamping the approval of this said rarity
Clarifications bestowed upon one another
Being straight forward could never be more appreciated
No reason to display fallacies to the new accepting eye
First impressions upon thy mind
On one's best behavior
No foolhardy comments or haughty gestures
Mentally searching for a reason to further the potential situation
For future encounters
Nothing is promised between the two.
No expectations –
Just pure attraction and open minds.

Thoughts of time being wasted
Getting down to the point often run the mental streams of the participants
But in all honesty time will only tell the destiny of this first encounter.

A LETTER TO LOVE

I thought you taught me how to love
Even though you came at a time when I wasn't looking for love
Mentally wrapped me around your finger
Made me feel like I was nothing without you
I depended on your love because it filled so many dark places with light in my heart.
Love can't explain what our connection taught me.
When I would be with you, every problem in the world, in my eyes, I was blinded to.
Sitting watching movies, looking at you cook dinner in your wife beater and booty shorts
Talking about our past and where we would love to go in the future
Discussions of puppy love – would you die for me? I would die for you…
But it alluded so much more to our complex utopia.
Yearning for your love and just knowing that you are satisfied
Looking you in your eyes and wondering what can I do better each and every single time
Never letting you have a moment to question whether I cared for you
I struggled – you struggled, and we both faltered in our relationship.
I sought counsel through friends that have been through similar situations and still made it,
But it was our pride, trust issues, and doubt that guarded our purity from each other.
No one person is as perfect as the next.
No wrong is greater than the next, but maybe our selfish ways
We calculate a new equation of how sin is produced and judged.

All this to say that I know you are the one for me.

Your threats and recent decision to really let this be,
It baffled me.
My head felt stuffed, and I began to have a hardening of breath.
My vision got blurry.
My adrenaline began to rise.
My legs felt weak and my arms began to feel heavy.
None of my thoughts were clear -
Mind racing with what is really occurring.
Imitations of drunken responses to friends when the phone is answered,
But cannot accurately portray the hurt with my sobriety.
People looking at me with the same dumb ass question: Are you ok?
Of course fucking not, I want to ball up and watch movies with Dodges

Chicken until I can answer: Why?
Why now of all times?
Why not back when I was truly not looking for love?
Why did you walk…
Better yet, why did you welcome yourself into my life by sitting in my lap that night?
I didn't need you in my life then,
But you walk out at a time when you are most needed.

Pain is weakness leaving the body, and for so long we have been apart from each other now,
And I still honestly would have to tell the truth and say that I'm still in love with you.
I do not want to be and would truthfully love to get over you, but I cannot.
I got the shitty end of the pole stick here.
I walk around and hold my chest up high and act as if I'm not stressing with the depressors of my soul.
When did it really do it for you?
I sat around while you gave up on our relationship for months
Dealt with your insecurities and doubts
Kept the spark alive the best I could,
And still you say I failed you.

One of my greatest fears is the fear of failure.
How in the world will I get over this?
Fucking, smoking, drinking cannot promise me a safe recovery
Just medians running their course back to reality.
How I feel towards you won't even allow me to experience someone else's true affection.
I cannot visually see into their hearts.
I cannot sense their being merging with my own.
It is incapable do too the intertwined genetic makeup we have created.
It would behoove you to recognize this one-day
None of my previous relationships have felt like this.
Guess this is one of the cons of growth.
Growing when you don't want to leave a chapter in your life
Turning over the next leaf
Moving in motion when no force has influenced the energy
Matter that is frozen being forced to its polar opposite
All this I know you would understand if not no one else would.
We always were able to have an intelligent conversation
Play nerdy games of simple corrections on speech and grammar
Black berry merlot, dinner, and a movie with plans of some intense late-night

activity
Simply just you and me.
My longing for you now is an addition that I can longer fight to mend.
When push comes to shove, I'm starting to let it go.
Turning the other cheek when your negative words strike.
You sucked the fight out of me.
We share the same monologue for each other.
A mirror separates you from me
Fuck the judging parties – I'm independently in love with thee.
Walking out could have never hurt me any worse.
A monster was created from this beautiful relationship.
The intentions on this being was not intended
Grendel hears my cry through his sensitive ears
Shakespeare couldn't write this love story.
The King of Oxford, the true poet behind Romeo and Juliet,
Could not fathom the words to describe our love and put it in a stanza.
Critical responses from history lessons don't tell you how to love.
Biblically, it describes a BEING who is the ultimate lover but even HE gave
Eve to Adam for the sake of companionship.
Ain't no player's club what love got to do with it misconceptions in this
This is the waiting to exhale, Tristan and Isolde, letter of love.
There are not enough words or lines in this notebook to truly express what
you mean to me.
So as a battery slowly losing its juice,
A marker running out of fluid
Or simply a life coming to an End.
This is my analytical funeral for you.
And now I have fallen out of verbally being in love you.

One....

One of my greatest fears is the fear of
failure.
How in the world will I get over this?
Fucking, smoking, drinking cannot promise me
a safe recovery
Just medians running their course back to
reality.

HEAR MY CRY

MY CRY TO CULTURE

MY BLACK IS

Pressed against the walls of oppression
Clenched fist – bruised knuckles
Blood dripping on the warm sweaty threads
MY BLACK IS…
Exhausted mentally – frustrated from the hours call of duty
Walking amongst those who may not fully comprehend
MY BLACK IS…
Eyes watching thine every move – waiting on the explosion from within
Pushed and shoved and verbally stoned with hatred
MY BLACK IS…
Atomic bombs igniting the fury within put at ease as the deep breath calmly
released with the smoke from turning the other cheek
MY BLACK IS…
Monstrous thoughts and actions that could arise from this endangered
species.
MY BLACK IS…
Boiling with anger – temptation of quarrels presents themselves taunting the
human feelings
MY BLACK IS…
Jolts of pain sought out for collection – high committees purging upon the
minstrel savages – stretched across a sea of corrupted utopias balance on the
backs of scum
STILL…
We stand clenched fist and bruised knuckles with a hope that still reigns
supreme

MY BLACK IS

<u>BROTHERS</u>

There is no difference between you and me.
Same struggle – different hustle
A brother from identical situations
Follower of different crowds
Still speak aloud the same Invictus
Out of the night shining armor we patrol this twisted world

Where art thou good brothers?
Hidden behind diverse organizations -
Hidden behind private obligations -
Souls tied down my personal endeavors -
Why do us brothers stray away from our true creed?

Vampires and leeches are the antagonist to our melting pot of society
The push to our pull
This is my plea to my real brothers.
Regardless of who you are…
Where you are…
What you are…
It is our duty to change this godforsaken hell bound bloodsucking life
diminishing Grimm reaping world.
I stand but WE need to pull ourselves up by the bootstraps
And let the pettiness of the man, homogenous beefs, and false critical avatars
that cannot be us GO!

Until the end of time, this needs to be our anthem.

I rest my case…

Where art thou good brothers?
Hidden behind diverse organizations -
Hidden behind private obligations -
Souls tied down my personal endeavors -
Why do us brothers stray away from our true
creed?

HEAR MY CRY

BROKEN & BEATEN

Swollen ankles
Shackled with rusted iron
Backs filled with sweat, blood, and crumbs of earth
Muscles exposed to the air - flesh exposed
Battered and wrinkled faces
Faces of despair and hopelessness
Governed by the white ghost
Commands that degrade the pride of a man stripped from freedom
Cultivated into a subculture
Spiritual hymns reign on the hour
As the sun clocks 12 in the sky
The overseer thrust his whip
Cottonmouth floods the field
Brainwashed settles within the minds of the sieged
Dysfunction crawls amongst the shacks
Rumors of escape and false hope
The sweet taste of that young Negro girl's innocence
Devoured by the white ghost at the nightfall
Only to be risen at the sound of the horn
And a young boy watching his father be hung.
Cycles of blood shed across the south
The wheat sings with the voices of our ancestors.
Wooden boxes filled the grounds of plantations.
Civil disobedience sentenced to 150 lashes
The slave mind crashes
Boiled with anger
Eyes of darkness
The inner animal is created
Suffering from chronic mistreatment
Overlapped punishments
Burden the runaways
Dreams of the underground railroad
That "Great getting up in the morning"
All long for the story of Solomon Northup
But most fair to the judgement of Master
Decades past, history changes:
Martin's dream was adapted.
Malcom's revolt was not in vain.
Marcus Garvey's cry was heard.
Huey Newton's character now fills the mind of African- American's offspring.

Maya Angelo's words strike the heirs of nations; but yet if you look within our society's flaws, we still have only created new slaves.

BLACKBOY

So, I am walking to the corner store in Alabama
Visiting my grandfather.
I had just got through playing basketball, so I was a little thirsty.
As I was walking into the store, a white woman and her son were exiting.
As I got closer, she pulled her son close as I proceeded into the store. They
walked away quickly.
Her look was not the least bit warming or accepting.
Still in a good mood, I ignore the small shit.
But I feel a ghostly presence behind me.

One aisle over there's two pair of sky-blue eyes staring at me.
Soon the figure moved toward me and asked how may he help me.
Thinking that he is providing great customer service, I reply "No thank you,
sir."
Then, he refuses my answer, and this time it hits me!
"Boy look at me," he says. "How may I help you?"
Eyes widen, heart beats furiously
No time to think, but thoughts of what I should do – is all that filled me.
So many actions being planned out mentally, but physically I am rock solid
like a statue,
So what to do?

Decades past, history changes:
Martin's dream was adapted.
Malcom's revolt was not in vain.
Marcus Garvey's cry was heard.
Huey Newton's character now fills the mind of
African- American's offspring.
Maya Angelou's words strike the heirs of
nations; but yet if you look within our
society's flaws, we still have only created
new slaves.

HEAR MY CRY

WHAT IS A DREAM?

What is a dream?
If you walk in the midst of the unknown
Neither fact nor fiction
Our future has yet to be filled
In the present we speak life into existence
Trampling the thought of death
But yet our dreams sometime reflect upon our past
Dangerous minds have the most beautiful structure
Thoughts of misfortune brought unto mankind
Outweighing the imaginary climax of our youth
Television feeding into our minds plotting the birth of the next generation of
terrorists
Blocking pathogens to create success
Born into crooked systems programed for their demise.

What is a dream?
Left forgotten for so long
Life hits one so hard
Dreams leave us not to believe.

One aisle over there's two pair of sky-blue
eyes staring at me.
Soon the figure moved toward me and asked how
may he help me.
Thinking that he is providing great customer
service, I reply "No thank you, sir."
Then, he refuses my answer, and this time it
hits me!
"Boy look at me," he says. "How may I help
you?"
Eyes widen, heart beats furiously
No time to think, but thoughts of what I should
do – is all that filled me.
So many actions being planned out mentally,
but physically I am rock solid like a statue,
So, what to do?

HEAR MY CRY

BLACK SHEEP

Lyrical embellishments swallowed by the soles of the rejected
Collaborations with the voices of sorrows, hearts being sold at pawn shops
rented out on borrow
Hollow introductions producing tail ended produce
Wavelengths read by the dead
Red beams on dilute
Failed polygraphs
Infractions collapsing
Retracting included on meters of deception waiting to be collected by the
grim patron
Standing at the position of attention stiff in limbo
Parade at rest
Eyes of March
Carbohydrates kicking into starch
Energy freed from utopia feels
Yielding the iron arch
Joint banners trampling the toes of protesters
Weird words working wonders without world of war washing widowed
women with the white written wraths wrapped within warts…
Left to the cities court
Genius minds form Colts
Opportunist in forms of opponents

Let me explain— the males replace women in feministic behaviors
Let me dumb it down
Niggas talk more than bitches these days…

Relinquishing trusted competition but in rebukes the true nature of the being,
which is to leave you fucked
So, you say you feel me, but you won't feel me until you've been socially
crucified
Reborn on a throne of horns
A past that was on crash
40-yard dashes of lashes struck by tongues of whores
The gore from young bulls attempting to ram my red cape
Taped mouth's that are diamond infested
Burnt edges creased secured by the deceased …
Just to taste the blood that drips from my feet, walking a path of destruction
thoughts of self-demolition my spirit rejects in a rescue form
Because of my religions crooked laws.
My darkest talents remain hidden.

Next time you see me remember my words
Mirrors reflecting images manifest upon the herds.
Black sheep unite!

BLACK HISTORY

An educated black man is posed as a dangerous thing.
I'm a Red Bull – attached nose ring but I can't be pulled
Yield at the most opportune moment
But my tank is on FULL, thumbs bruised from rubbing the RULE
40 acres and a MULE, and an extra mile – that's some BULL
From the colorless hands beaten and shaken down (so cruel)
Spitting image of our cultures
Burden shoulders, splintered hands
Anger combined with fear rattling coasters
Traveling and stealing from the natives the true west coasters
Top of the rosters looking at the blue-eyed monster
Standing on a stilt frozen cold getting clocked in.
Sons losing fathers – daughters becoming emotional martyrs
Mothers left to become double parents
Chained and tagged while being out on clearance
Homogenous gender and race crimes
Began mentally and socially with Uncle Tom
Bomb…blown into sickness at harm.
Comparatives…sound the alarm
Man versus self
Men versus race
Man versus society
Simply complexions of complexion
Sunday law to Martial Law are the predecessors to the Jim Crow law
Blocked in blocks stacked on – snatched from our own fields of free
governments
An organized movement
Screams of Willie Lynch for president
Black vote for Huey Newton – top candidate for his assassination
President Nixon the father of Luther
Porcelain needles and stragglers on rooftops
Young blacks imitating cops and robbers
Look at the psychological images being digested
Imposters from times of times ago
This is my poetic justice.
Our legacy brewed from the saliva of ancestors
Referred dreams like Hughes and Hoover
Plural representatives of speech and violence
Reviving shattered culture from dried blood and soulless restrictions
Let's bring the war of freedom to doorsteps making this relevant
That we still struggle economically from this democracy

Let me explain– the males replace women in feministic behaviors
Let me dumb it down
Niggas talk more than bitches these days...

HEAR MY CRY

Soliciting to our brother and sisters that relief is in these trees
Socially tormented through video perceptions and false advertisement of an
American dream on TV
Education systems failing drastically
HBCUs losing accreditations
Only 6 degrees removed by terrorist live amongst our race and families
Brothers catching heat from sisters
Only if they knew that was developed from slavery too
None of this is to blame THE MAN
Just motivation to get an education and make a difference
Use my gifts- use my voice to connect to the spirts of those around me
Move the crowd and not to sway their judgements
But to spread the awareness
That the fight is still on
Justice has yet to be completely fulfilled
So, I stand as a resistance
A descendent of a field Negro
And
Still I RISE

Soliciting to our brother and sisters that
relief is in these trees
Socially tormented through video perceptions
and false advertisement of an American dream
on TV
Education systems failing drastically
HBCUs losing accreditations
Only 6 degrees removed by terrorist live
amongst our race and families
Brothers catching heat from sisters
Only if they knew that was developed from
slavery too
None of this is to blame THE MAN
Just motivation to get an education and make
a difference

HEAR MY CRY

A FLOWER ONCE BLOSSOMED

Polished nails
Blunted and bloody tips
Boxes behind sender blocks
Airtight facility
A thunder erupts in her lungs
Ultra-soft cotton dresses
Ripped and torn
Drowned in sweat
Drenched in installation pieces
She contemplates giving up
Still her grip is firm wood breaking skin
Drinking the blood of her fingertips
Hair entangled on the rusted nails
The hair on neck raises
A small breeze of hope released from her lips
Sounds of wheels passing by on the wet streets
No one in her faint sight near to hear her grasp for help
Running clips of shattered memories
Chalked out position of her body lays trembling
A flower once fully blossomed
Battered and beaten
The moonlight shines down upon her
Time passes her relentlessly
Forest fires of emotions overflow inside of her
She closes her eyes and falls asleep
In her darkest hour
The mornings dew rests upon her cheeks

Justice has yet to be completely fulfilled
So, I stand as a resistance
A descendent of a field Negro
And
Still I RISE

HEAR MY CRY

WARS AND BUTTERFLIES

Nothing is the same in our world today
Running in circles on hot coals
Spreading disease to the poor
Reluctant to serve the poor with the cure
But sell it to the crooked and twisted pure
Hell on earth glued to mental metal
Stained personality traits
Traits flooded with barbarian blood
Survival of the fittest
Springing into winter hearts
Juggle references of freedom inside the jungle
Fighting demon infested animals
Loose tongue, venomous words, rusted theories
Processed and projected for injection
This week's lesson on peace, nature, and violence
All of which coexist in time
Past, future, and present
Nobody knows how we got to the peace of butterflies
Totally forgetting the war and bloodshed
People depend on government and state rule
Such dysfunctional order
What about our roots of freedom amongst the wild?
Traded sin for a rifle and boots
Angel dust sprinkled on the nostril lining
Programming the peaceful for a war
Caterpillars stripped from cocoons forced early arrival
Stunted growth pumped with drugs
Monsters of society
Fairytale island under construction
Rumors of wars threaten our countries root function
Focus on world order instead of world peace
Simple theory of nature sightseeing watching the wild's heartbeat
Pulse is strong and healthy
Raw footage shot through tunnel vision
Mammals governing in technological deceit
Hierarchies set into place
Structure applied to each spectrum of life
Most grew in this world of wars and butterflies
This world of democracy
This world that is socially strapped with hot and cold climates
All that seems so negative

One broadcasted
Just take a second
A moment of nostalgia
Of a mid-spring day, a caterpillar transforms into a beautiful butterfly and
flies over the horizon avoiding all war in peace

THE AFTERMATH

When I look in those eyes of distress,
I grab onto the past tense.
Groups of messages temporarily pressed amongst my mental – lost focus of
the queen and lived in sin.
Trying to make matters end just as easy as actually making matter bend.
Acrobatics being practiced, searching for answers within linear equations.
Can't crack the calculus – stuck in the nucleus; the core strapped to the
hidden mathematics used to break my minds scientific method
Abused my happy home, dishonored my respective throne.
Simple transfer of illusions multiplied by the critical naked eye.
What could be so prodigal about these Black shackled politics?
Caught up on flags that are red instead of what needs to be read.
Mourning the deceased but we are no different if we don't protest, just a
walking dead.
I lack the cash to stop this bloodbath to come but have full access to the bath
salts that will numb the emotions from the revolution's aftermath.
Born on the nipple, puberty hits, stepped into the pool of vagina, teenage
years leave, reminiscing to old memories, looking forward I see a revolution
– bloodshed.
Pain and destruction of government, so I reflect. I'll look into the eyes of
distress and I grab on to the past tense…
We live in a world of snakes and crooked loyalist floating on the coast
awaiting the return of a true king.
The urge of power and control
Lords stand side-by-side in their shadows pending their chance of dreamt
rain – complete and total animalist natured I do not blame them – the heart
and soul of an alpha male.
One who has reigned and fallen into the same idle hands.
Locked into a frenzy of cruel intentions, how shall you rule again – by love
or hate in their demise?
Wounded in battle- slowly healing from scars internally

Caught up on flags that are red instead of what needs to be read.
Mourning the deceased but we are no different if we don't protest, just a walking dead.
I lack the cash to stop this bloodbath to come but have full access to the bath salts that will numb the emotions from the revolution's aftermath.

HEAR MY CRY

SOCIAL MEDIA

People die every day by social media.
Filling their brains with foolishness released by the press
And all conform to build a society of mentally suppressed
Kings and Queens shackled at the ankles caught up on DMs, comments, being Catfished, all types of different angles.
Inspector gadget tools built to rule the curiosity of the mind – caught up on who is dating or why someone left a suspicious emoji under a simple photo.
All this is being done and can't any of ya'll tell me what's going on in the healthcare reform.
What bills are being passed to screw our student loan repayment plans, or what the government is doing.
I mean, literally the baby boomers took books out our hands and gave us color television and electronics along with gaming systems while they control the true system of our generation.
The level of blindness is remarkable but sickening – to even know that even some of the people of our own generation have been conformed to this economical and political genocide.
People don't see what damage has been done.
Caught up on 15 second videos and rating games, but overlook videos of people dying in other countries and the rates of American soldiers dying overseas.
Relationships crumbling due to them scavenging through each other's photos inspecting the worst, assuming the thirst, but the truth is the dry mouth taste comes from the curiosity to seek
Spending too much time wondering what if and who's looking single and what you should be doing is working on your problems and strengthening your bonds with your significant other

All this to say...people...we need to wake up now!
And notice that there is more important things going on in the world.
Instead of following week to week the social feeds and seeing how many likes will put you in the lead
When you really need to lead your generation to spiritual salvation and political reform....
It's time for our generation to be reborn.

All this to say...people...we need to wake up now!
And notice that there is more important things
going on in the world.
Instead of following week to week the social
feeds and seeing how many likes will put you
in the lead
When you really need to lead your generation
to spiritual salvation and political reform....
It's time for our generation to be reborn.

HEAR MY CRY

NATURE NUMBER TWO

Abdominal pain with a gut strain
Back road running a maze of country filled with city limits – tobacco smoke blurs the GPS signal guiding the dim beacon across this field of illusion
Bruised brain cells
Trapped potential seeking answers in a game of chess.
Only it's lived by hours and days within weeks of trials governed by months of tribulations.
Tagged into years of memories locked by decades of past repetitions cycled through blood cells reproduced on the meters of compassion launched into orbit fused by the universe as we know it.
Overseers of supreme beings that tapped our consciences with the stingers of engine running organisms that will trace us and limit us, reaching dead end corners of life symmetrical rollercoasters
Birth it into a world of inventions and religious holograms that give us hope of an unknown salvation promised and passed down from oracle of time - Kronos
Stars fill the skies of our existence.
Polarized lenses polluting the visions of spirts that were created to save the souls of the lost
Parables written to tell the history, as we know it
Laws set into place to control our frontal lobe's ability to test the outcome of our futures.
Trapped in this maze of life, we stand defenseless under this democracy.
Lucid dreams come and go through the mainstream of tropical tsunami's that flood the gates to freedom.
Pensions posted to post of rigid wood surrounded with attempts to find the truth.
Mentally breaking bad with our own misunderstanding of how we came to truly be.
Leading to the waters of Jordan
Cured temporarily with hope.
Surrender to our doubt in the fact that this is it.
Ghost hunting the halls of death and the gift of life.
What is to come of our kind?
Mankind in the palm of time releasing the toxic euphoric gases into the sections of the globe.
Upon what hold are we really ruled by
Radically influenced – brain filled with curiosity – often judged and naturally the animalistic nature to fear those who threatened to go against the norm.
Those that refuse to settle for the world's order
When will this test end for us to transfer into phase 2?

Who will be the survivors to lead the next generation of existence to come?
There is more to this puzzle then we see, the pictures have hidden maps to
the ultimate truth
And who do we trust?
What is to come?
When is the capsule going to run out of sand?
How will we overcome?
Where will it lead us?
Something is coming and coming soon.
Wicked is good
Wicked game that is being played every time our body resets and wakes into
an atmosphere that can change at any moment.
The end is near.
This radical can sense it.
Are you ready?

THE HAND OF THE MAN

Hollowly pressed into the dark shade locked into position of distress
Shacked to the crest
And envy of the blessed
Anticipating the flex
Rekindling the site in the dimmed light frames
In fear of the claim
Restrain from the membrane
Juggling warfare bottomless mortars sounding the alarm of the heavens of thrones
Crammed in the crumbs of slums
Gorging stomachs with the acid of validity
Lack of responsibility in the masses of crashes interlocked with mental instability
Lost on this road of success
Publicly distorted images of spirituality
Legalization of affiliations demonized by the critics of biblical hierarchy
Anarchy amongst the poor
Depending on black glory
Foolery deceived as righteousness
Triumphing and trampling the elephants in the room
Processes into fixated zooms
Surging into the looms of forest fires
Acquiring the minds of the semantics
Running rapidly on treadmills bending the wheel of monstrous chords being played in today's radio spills
Lyrical janitors mopping up the mess of the thrilled
Internationally yielding the growth of cancerous overseers that are planting the seeds of our tomorrow…
Whispering in the feels of the unborn
 Scorned with the scarlet letters nailed to the post around the telecommunications threshold.
Standing bold on bricks emerged in water
Electrically wired with bombs of Salem
Realms of smoke filling the throats of the oppressed
Cries of wolves in the east
Jungle tamed hooligans run free in the west
Stars in the north surround the mounds in the east
Jungle tamed hooligans run free in the west
Stars in the north surround the mounds in the glitch of matrix
Slaughterhouse specials being grilled on the great tombs
Edgar Allan Poe in swift view

Twisted myths painted on the walls
In full strength the shame bleeds out into a karma sutra remix aftermath
After bath
Clash
Whipped with lavish lashes
Eyes beaten closed mind still on the task in constant fear of the casket
Bottle rockets of emotions blasted from the elastic
Tragic how the magic masks the howls from the wild
Looking for the Rite Aid in the pharmacy
Swimming alone in the lane subdued in the quickest sand laid by yet, the hand
of a man

<u>IMPROPER THOUGHTS</u>

The beginning is never the ending and the ending is never truly the end all be all

We fight for justice and freedom but lack the usual support of our government to look out for the people's best interest.

Waiting on changing guidance from above but our seats grow hot from sitting on the back burner, broken languages fill our streets.

The poor suffer, but our grocery stores are stocked with plenty working on our third depression.

Wall street has yet to learn their lesson.

Masked martyrs flood the gate of banks.

Relinquishing the security of financial stability of the rich and supplying the demand of nourishment to the community.

All this to say when will we unite as a people to demolish this country's burden

Rectify all government control and live amongst our own rule?

Back to our roots living in the marshes, running our fingers through grains of wheat.

Raising families, creating villages of purity, compare and contrast all the differences of how well this said democracy functions with the real world.

Everything is oblivion to the truth standing fast waiting on the approval of Congress.

While our government wages wars against countries.

Spoon-fed chemically induced substances drown in dysfunctional chaos, orange bliss, such a critical tactful taste of rumors spread into a world renown blooper

The beginning is never the ending and the ending is never truly the end all be all
We fight for justice and freedom but lack the usual support of our government to look out for the people's best interest.
Waiting on changing guidance from above but our seats grow hot from sitting on the back burner, broken languages fill our streets.
The poor suffer, but our grocery stores are stocked with plenty working on our third depression.
Wall street has yet to learn their lesson.
Masked martyrs flood the gate of banks.
Relinquishing the security of financial stability of the rich and supplying the demand of nourishment to the community.

HEAR MY CRY

EVOLUTION

Feeling like a little boy,
Chasing after my imaginary friend,
Leaving footprint tracks in the corridor
Smashing bubble wrappers in the mail
Swatting at flies in the kitchen
Quick hands-on catching mom's blue vase from falling,
Preventing a chaotic outcome,
Running around the house
Making endless noise.
Dad's calling out with a loud voice to stop acting like hoodlums
Mom follows through with the "Take the horseplay outside."
Stepping in the arena of multiple childhood games…
From curveball to hide and go seek, neighborhood youth all socialize
The beginning of the first real hierarchal order.
First fights, first best friend, first girlfriend, first job, first sexual encounter…
The first of monumental aspects of a human being's natural life.
Setting the standard high or low along the years of growth
So many lessons learned
Personality begins to form within
High school memories
Collegiate extravaganzas
Life experiences all mushed into one mold
A mold of a man who searches for a career
Success driven
Motivated from within family oriented and outgoing
Spending time in the community restoring civilized order
Spreading radical reform
Dreams of achieving wealth
Normal doubts of self
The dreaded feeling of being human.
The mind of our species complex but yet understanding
The now man of the household has intentions on growing old with his family.
Keeping the last name strong and alive
Offspring created in the cycle
Continues evolution

DAZE

Leaves falling
Living in autumn
Rearview mirror
Glazed over gaze
Distinct smell
Fresh burning incense
Rhythm of hip-hop
Ambulance for my imperfections
Natural Breeze
Sun powers my energy source
Constant repetition
Human nature
Free Spirit.

ABOUT THE AUTHOR

Calvin Ockletree is an author and entrepreneur. To support his endeavors or to book him for your book club event regarding this book, please email: trapofvibes@gmail.com